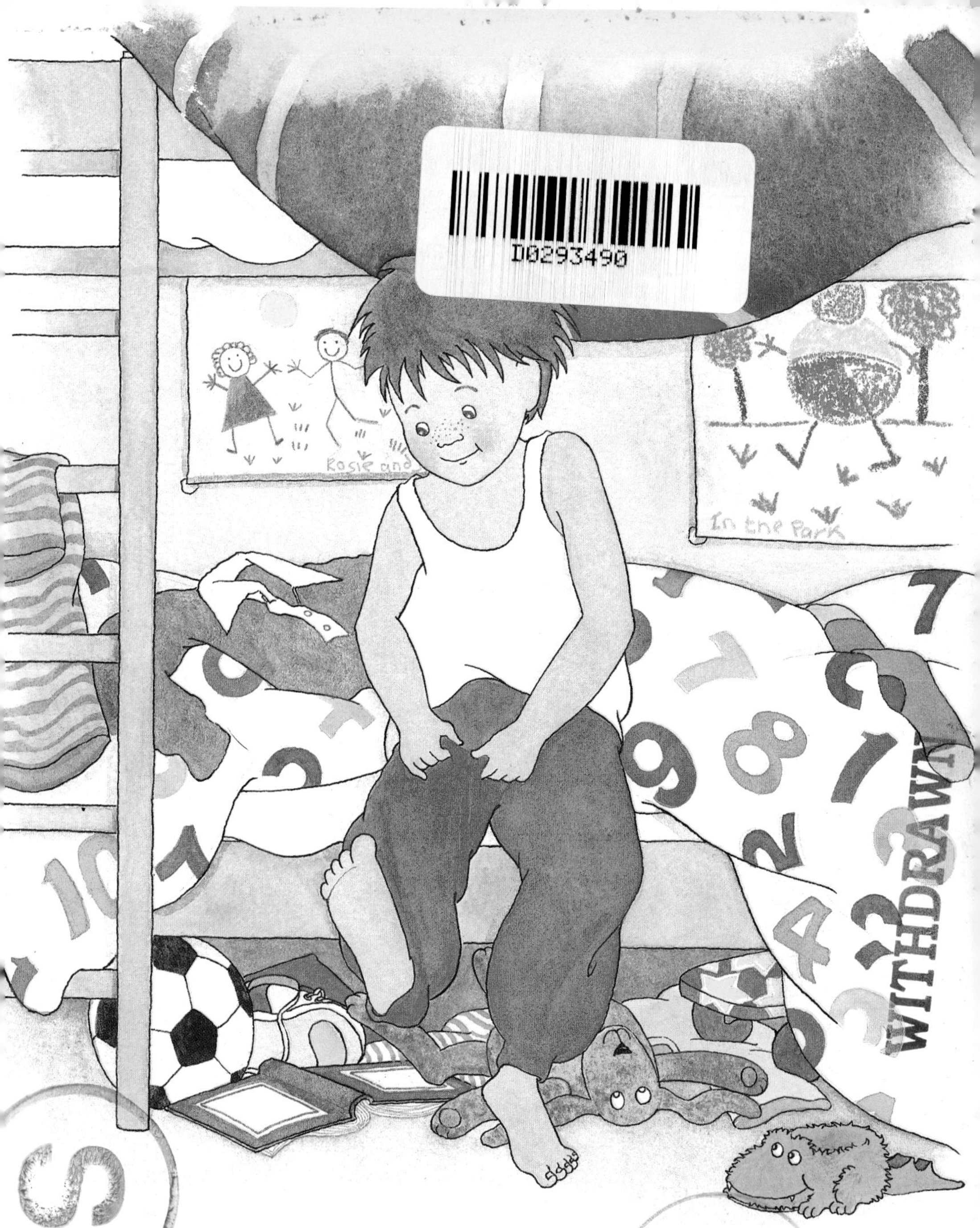

Sam was getting dressed.

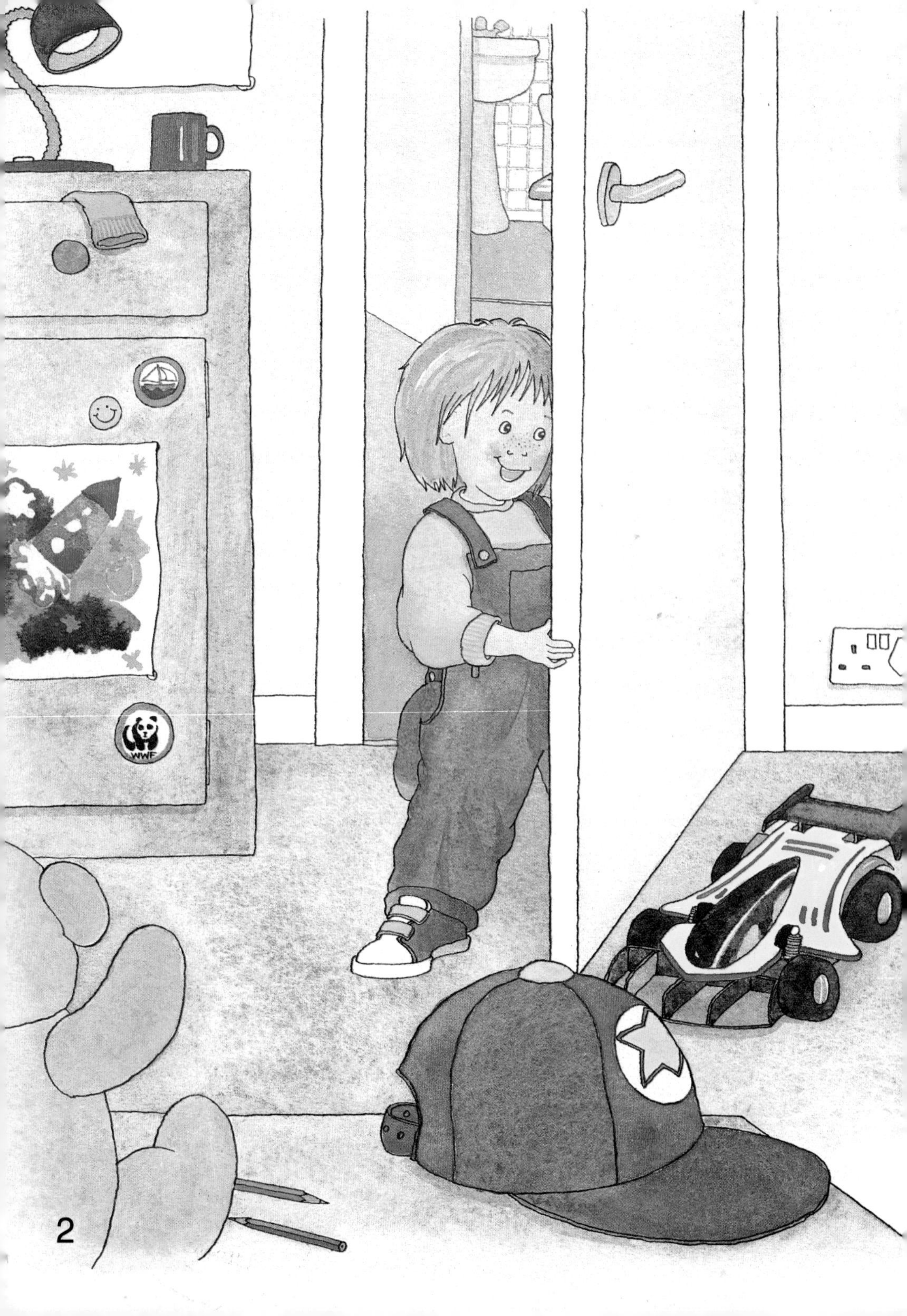
WWF

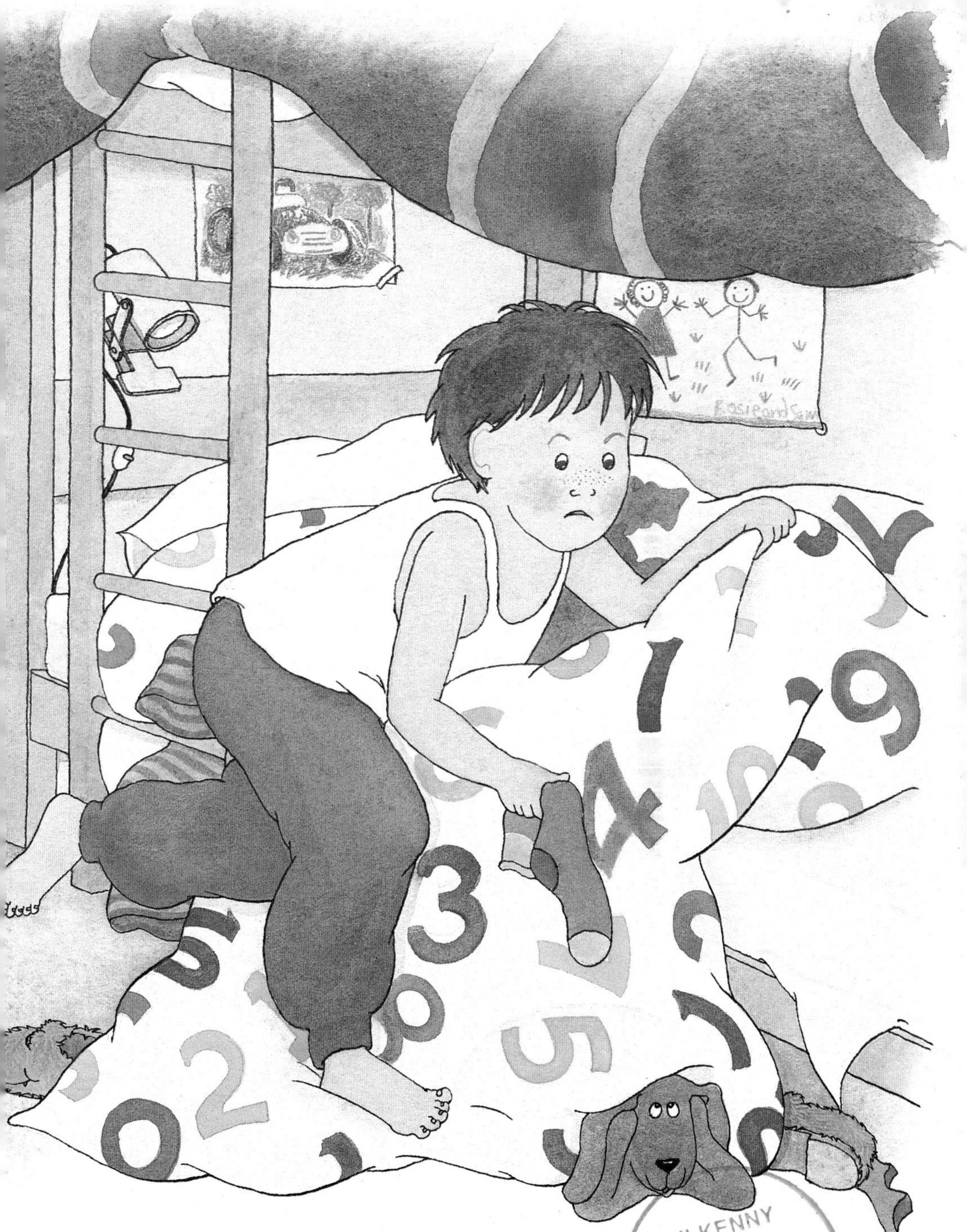

He had one sock.

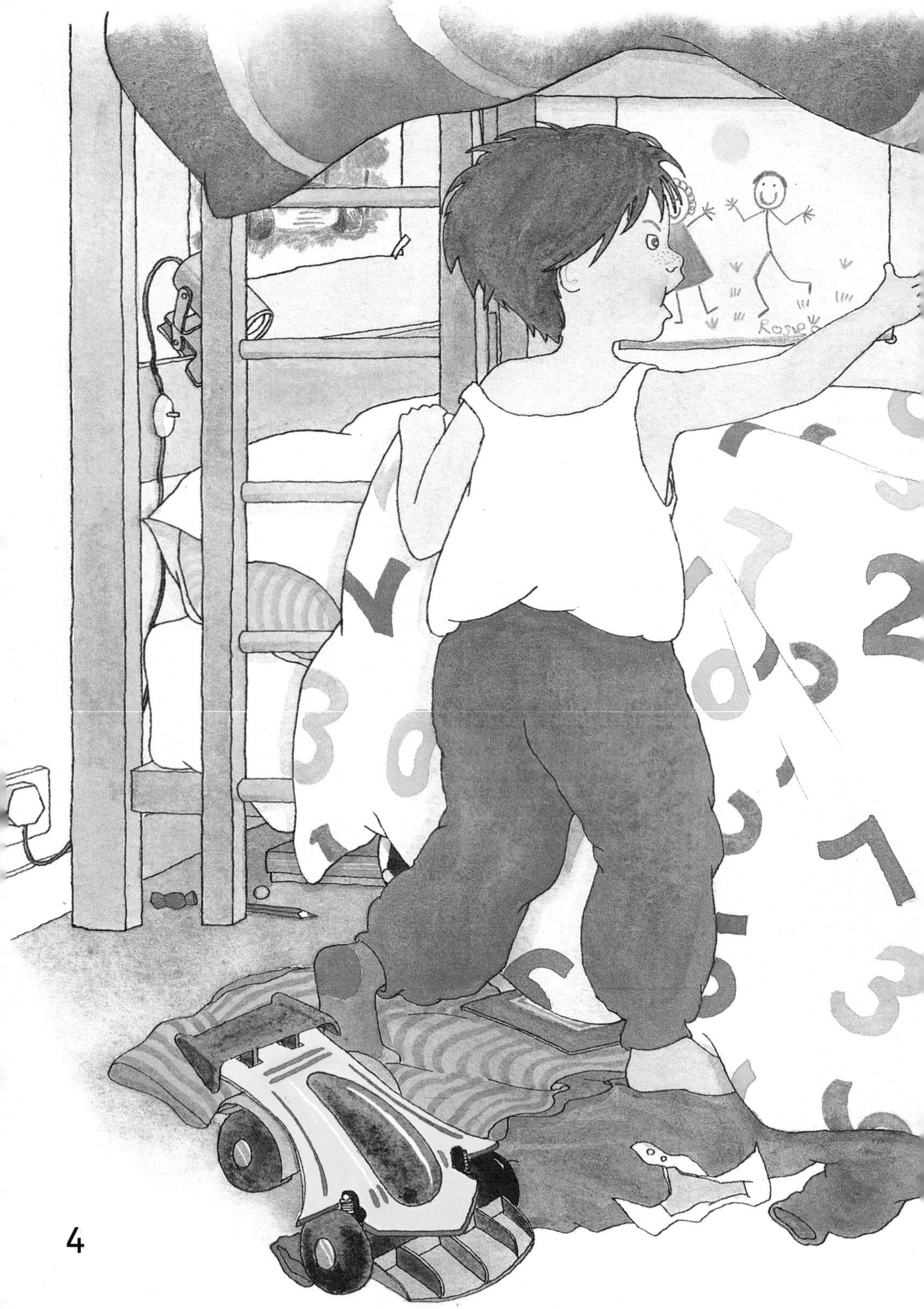
Rose

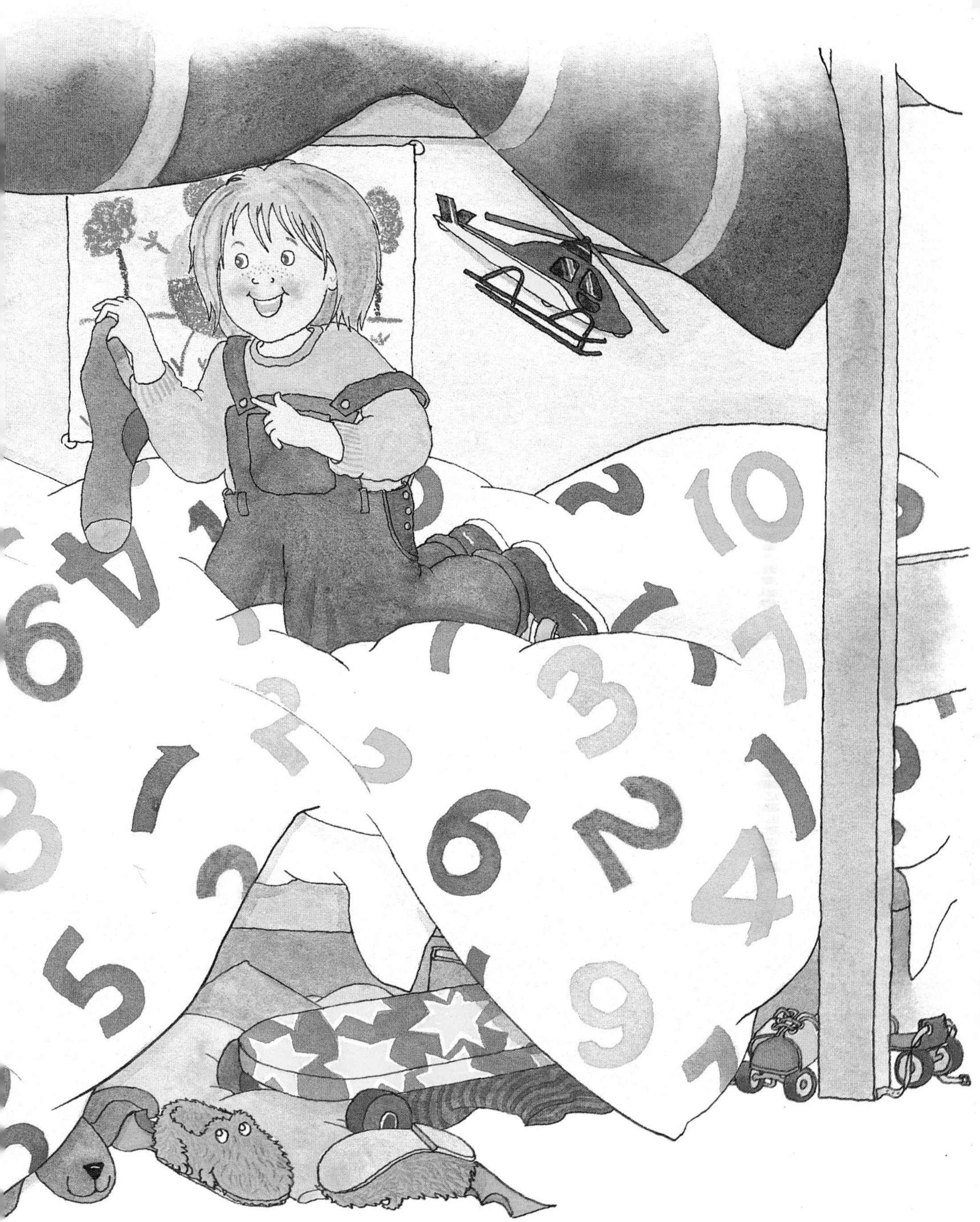

Lizzie laughed.

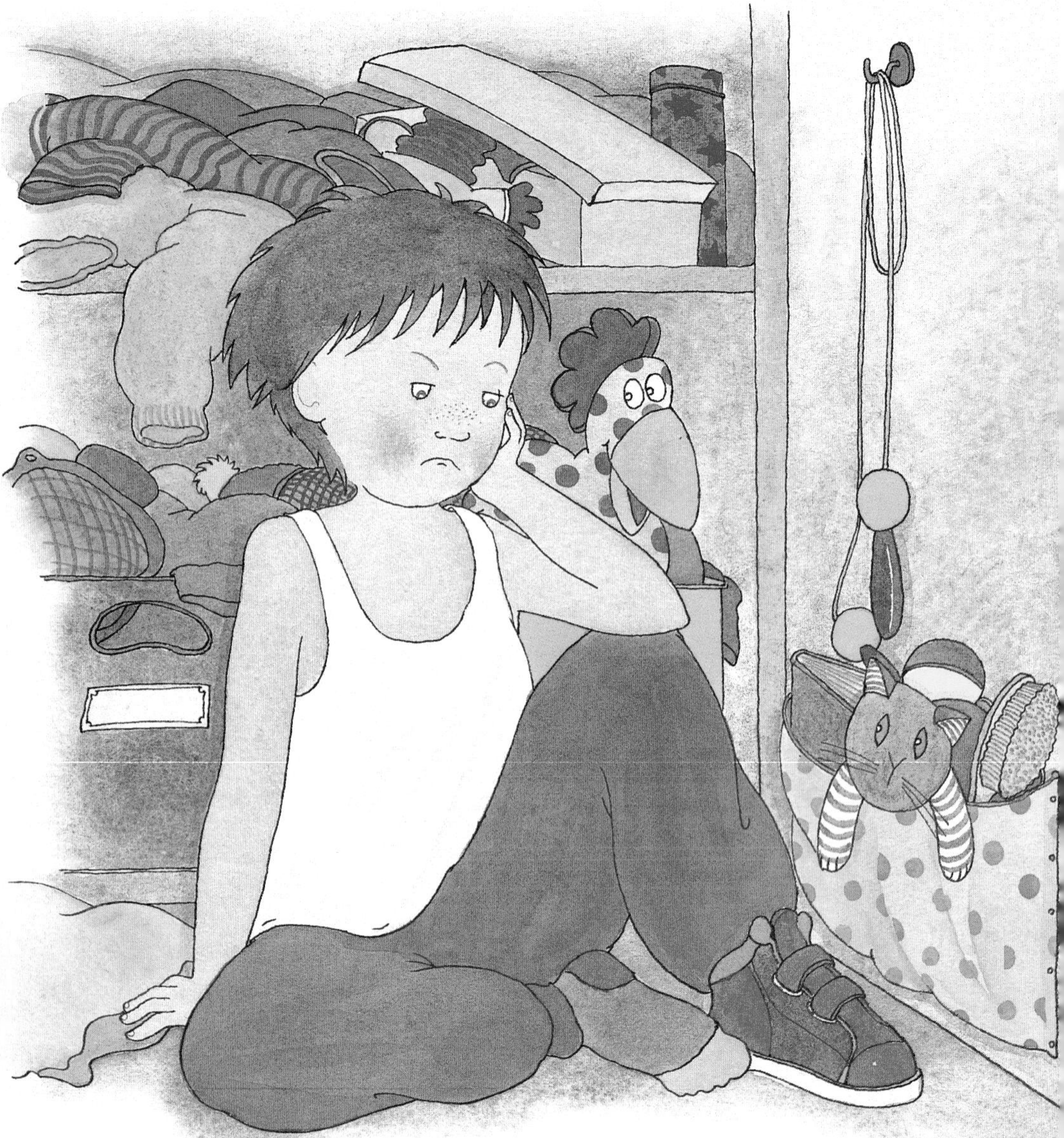

He had one shoe.

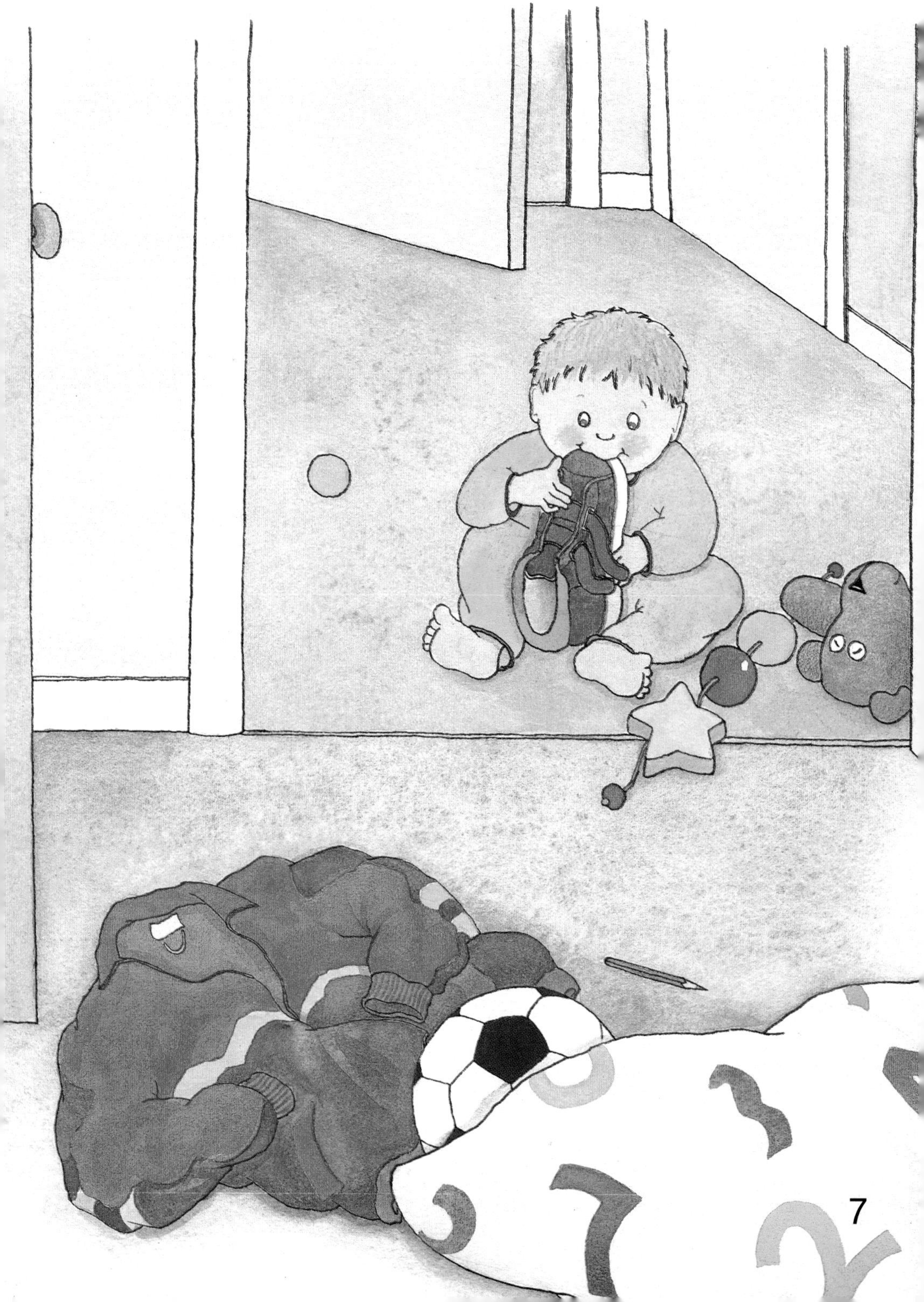

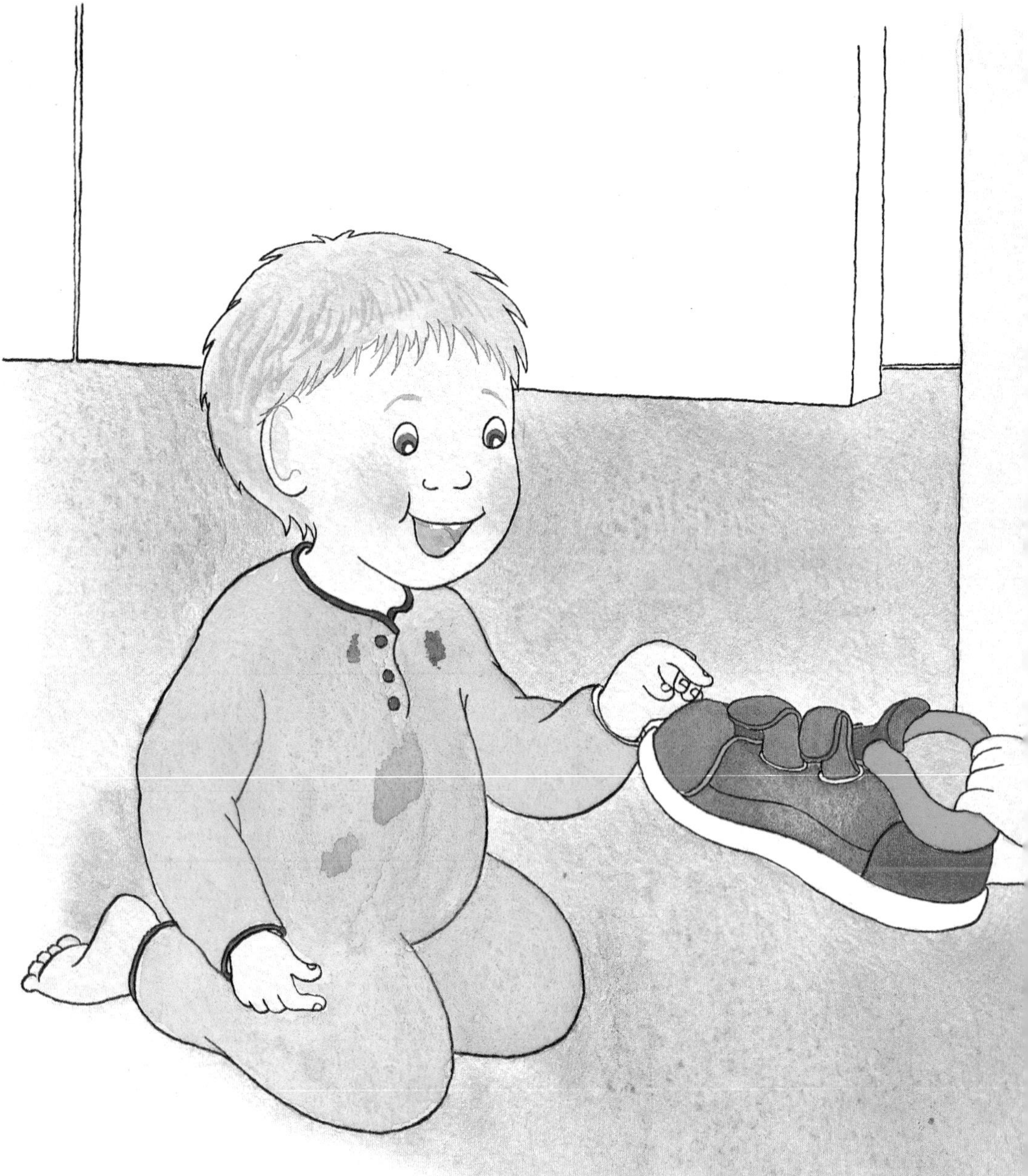

Jack laughed.

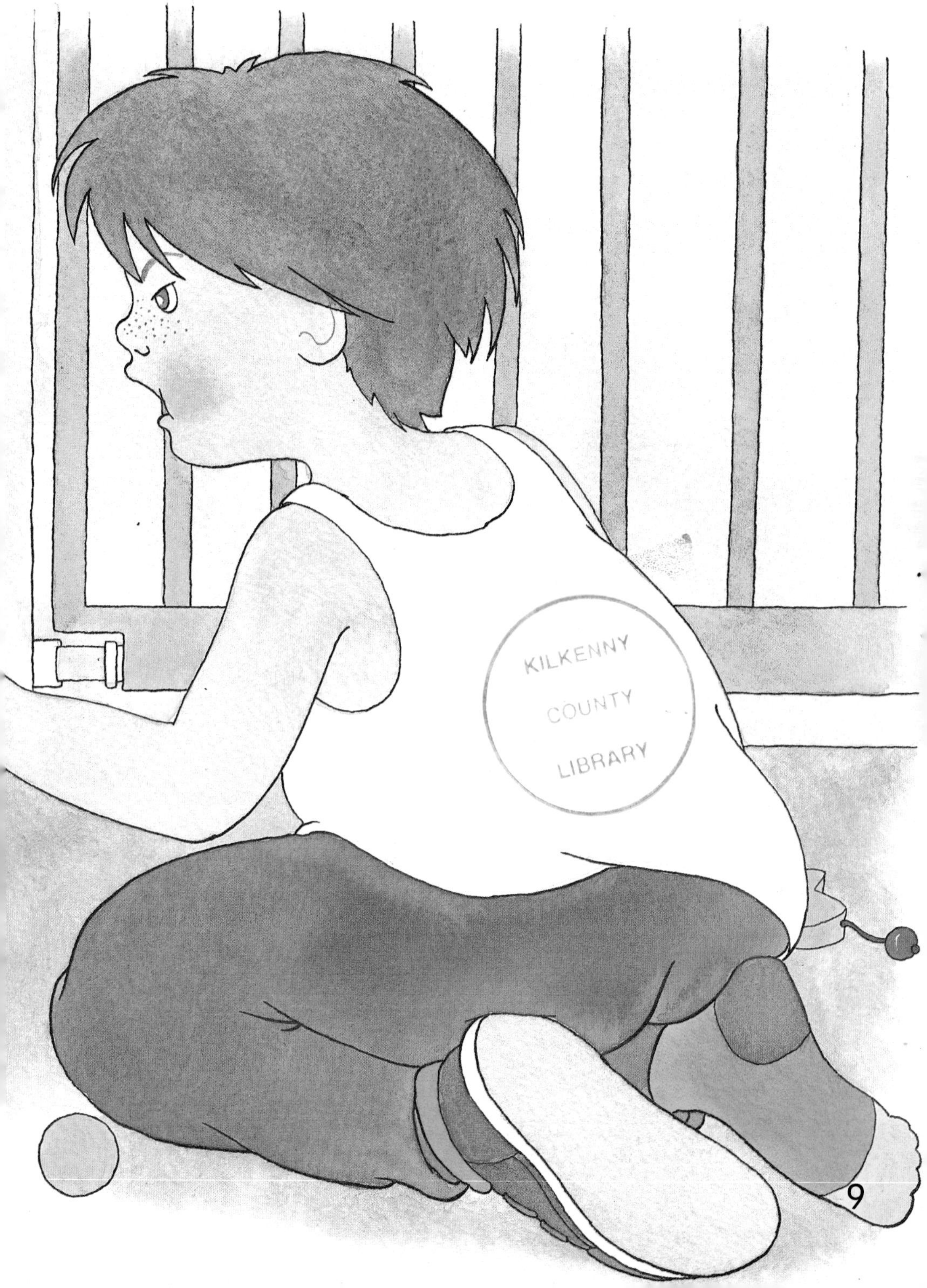

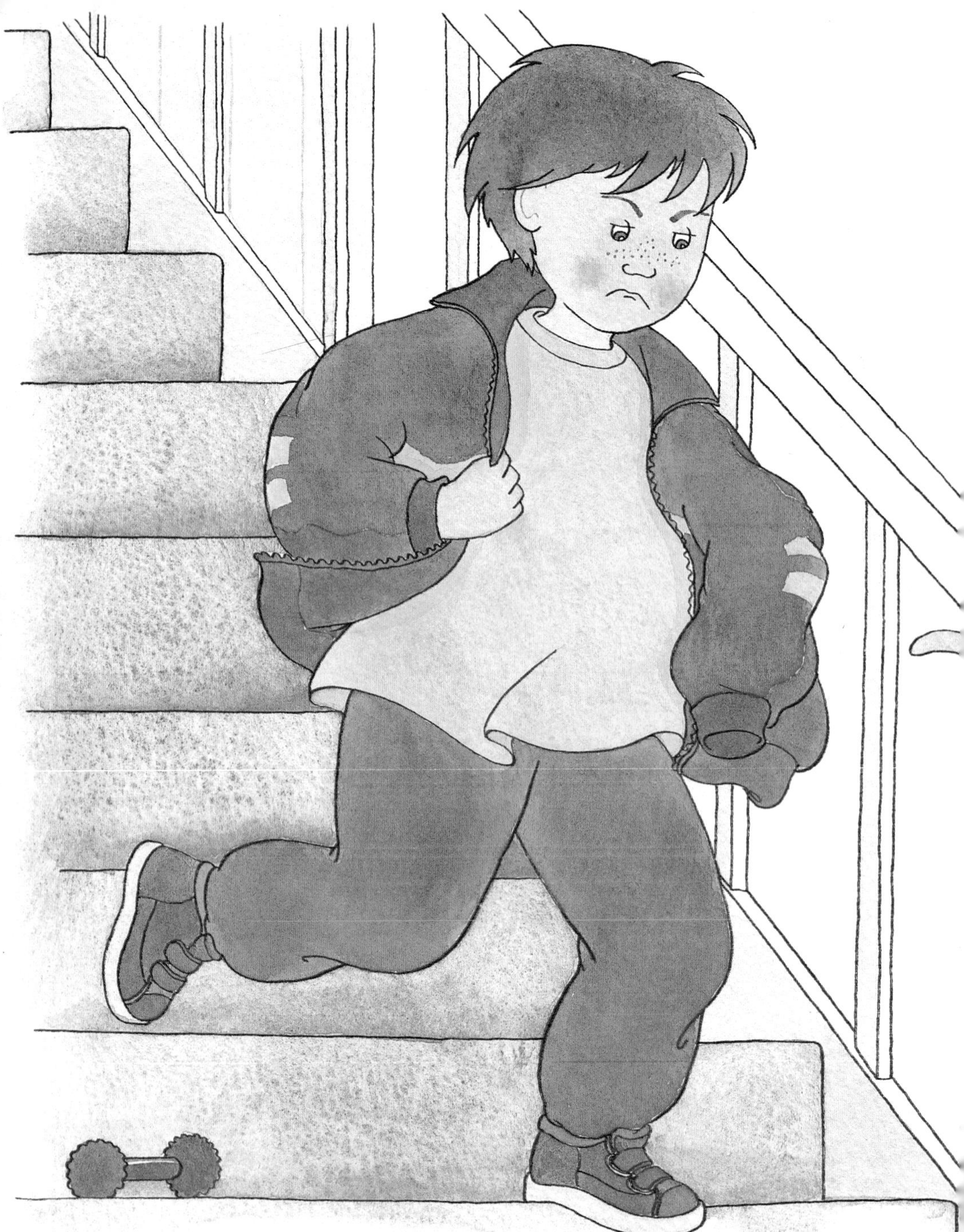

Sam was fed up.

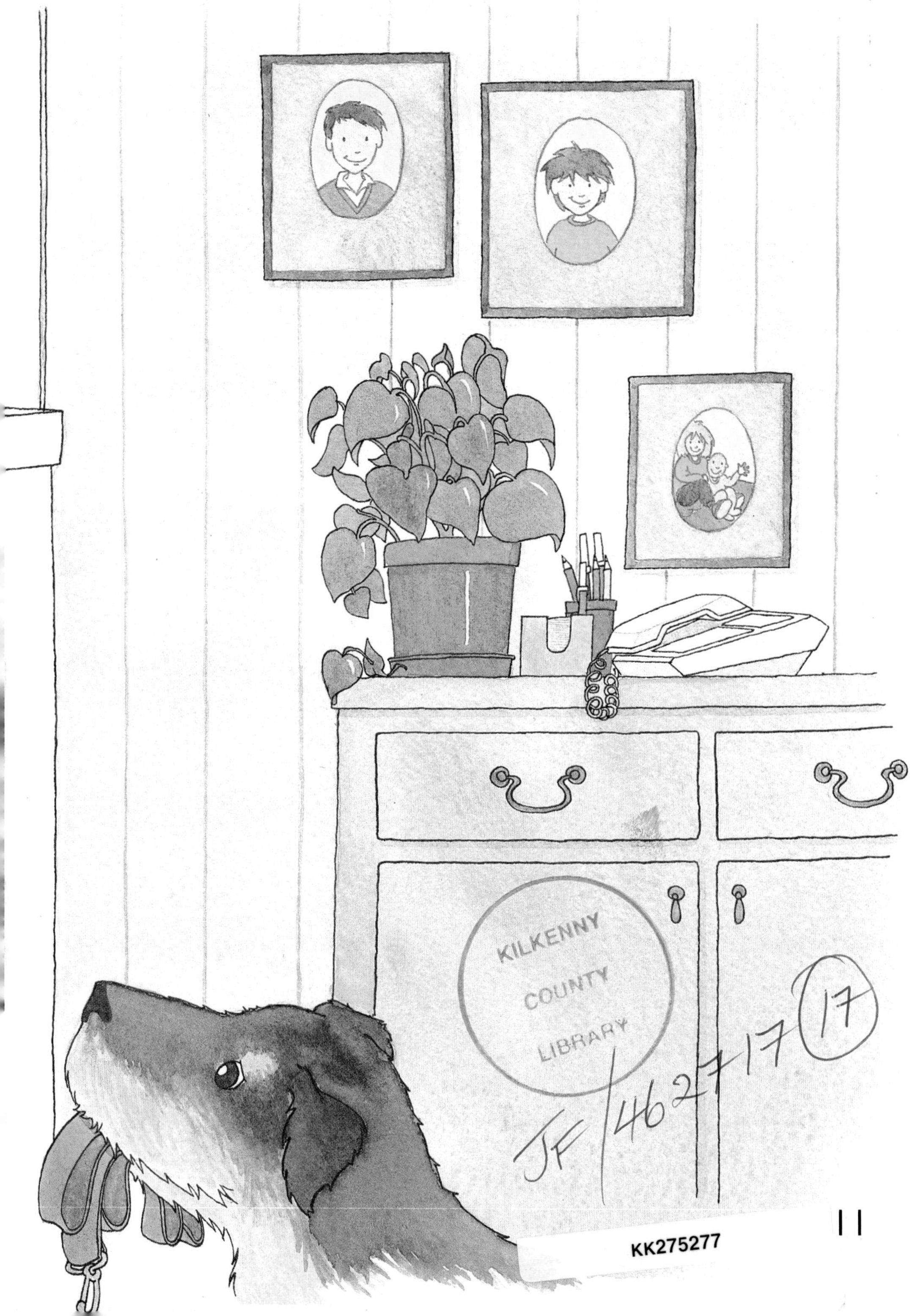

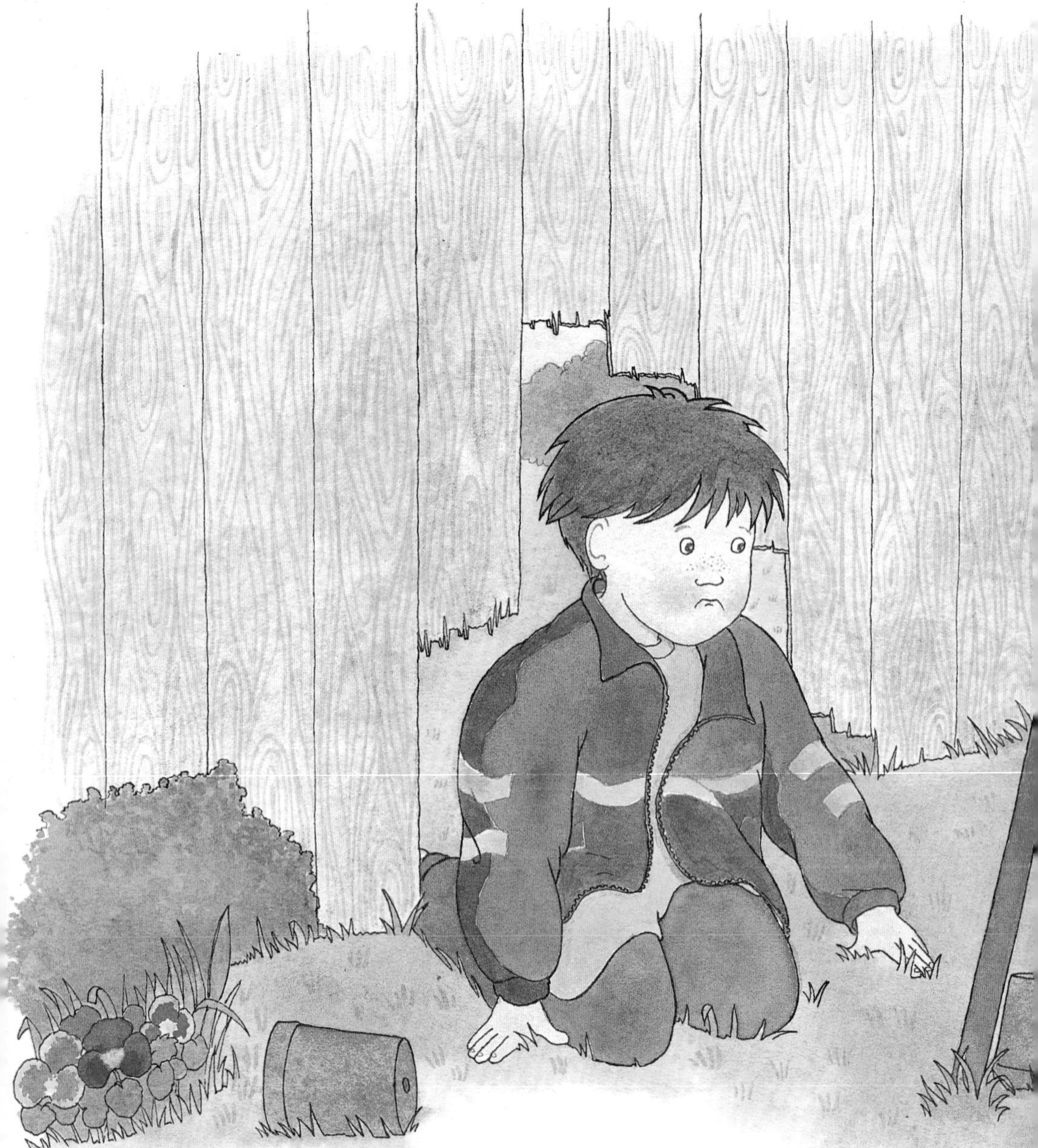

He went to see Rosie.

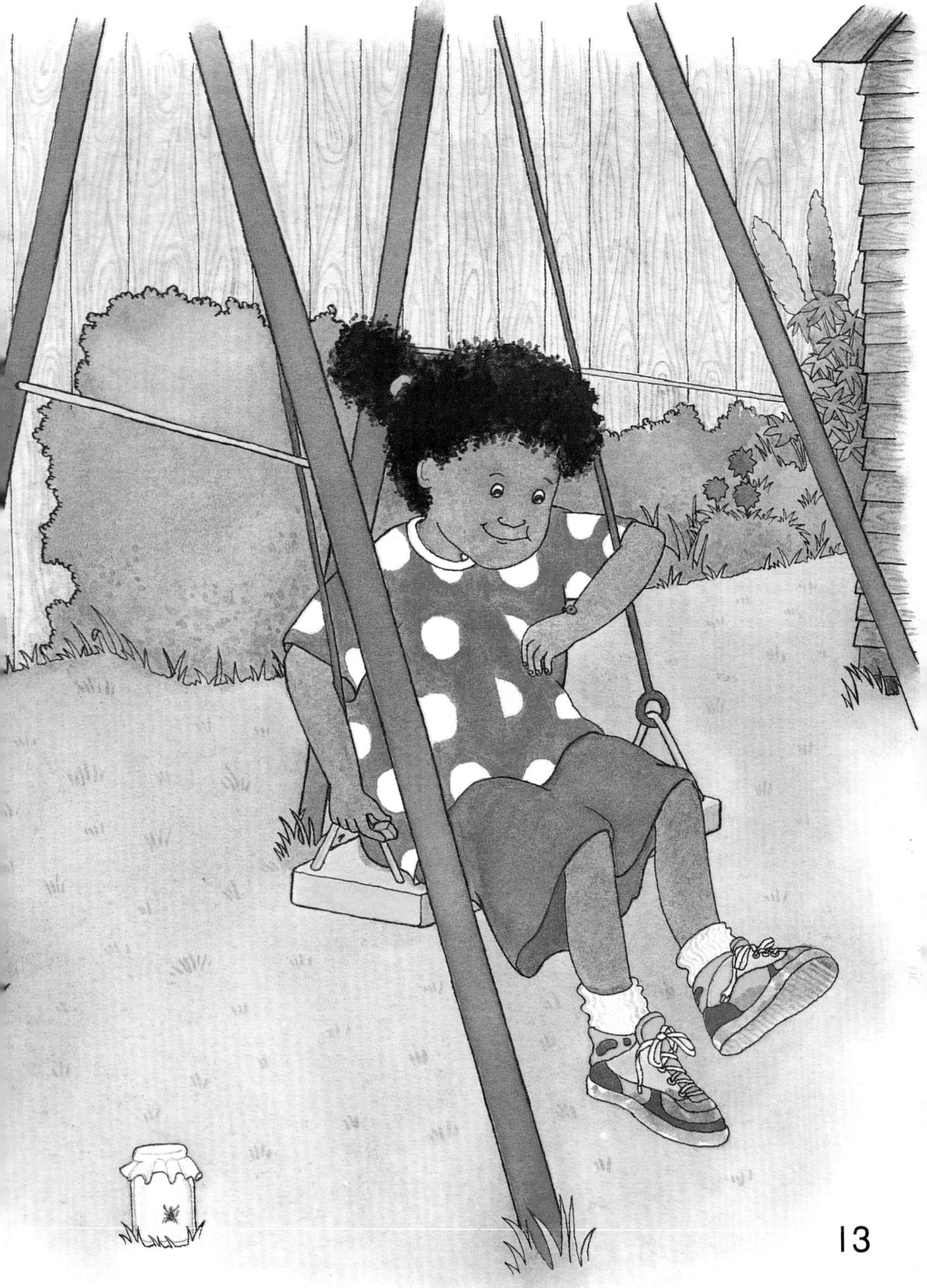

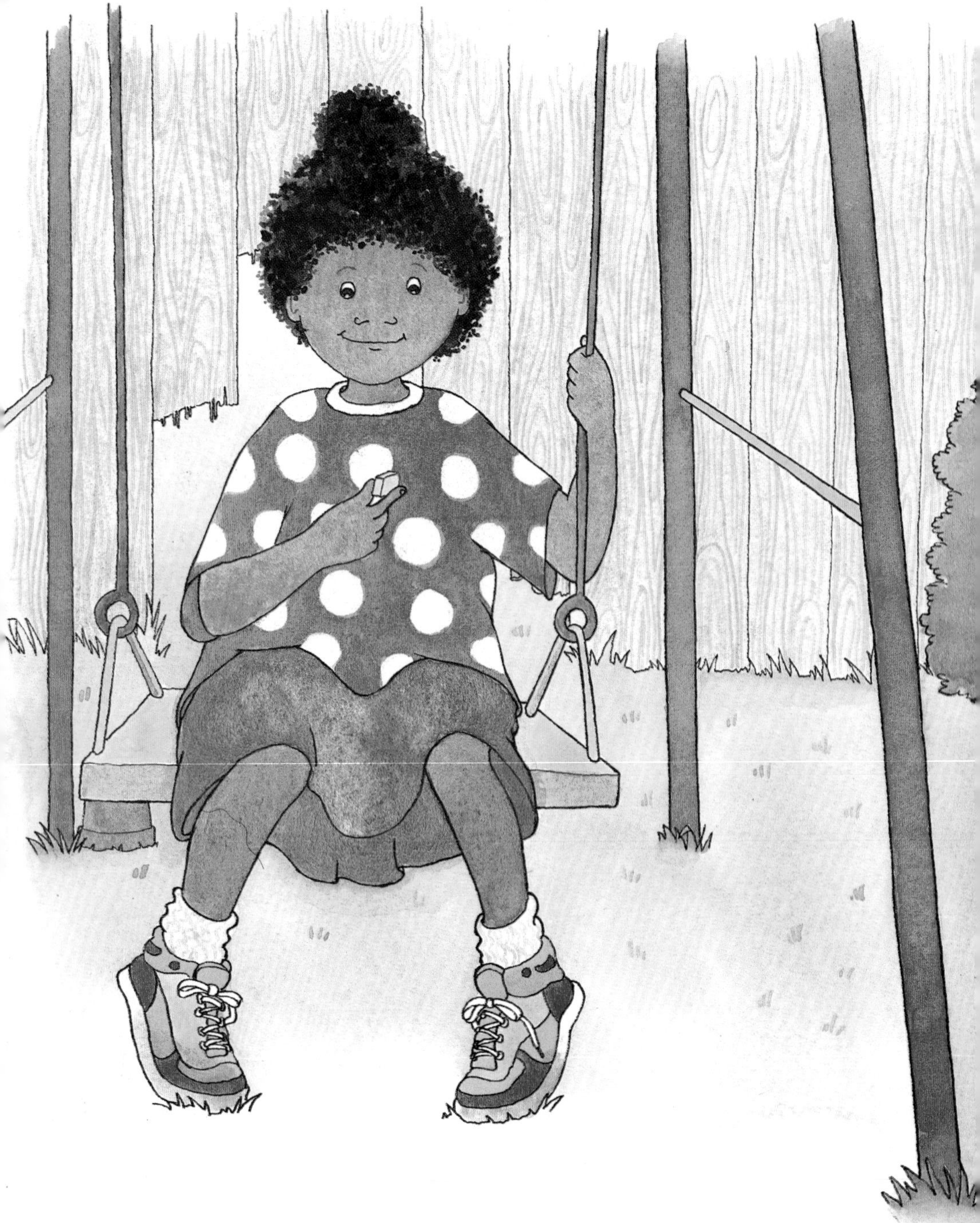

Rosie had one sweet . . .

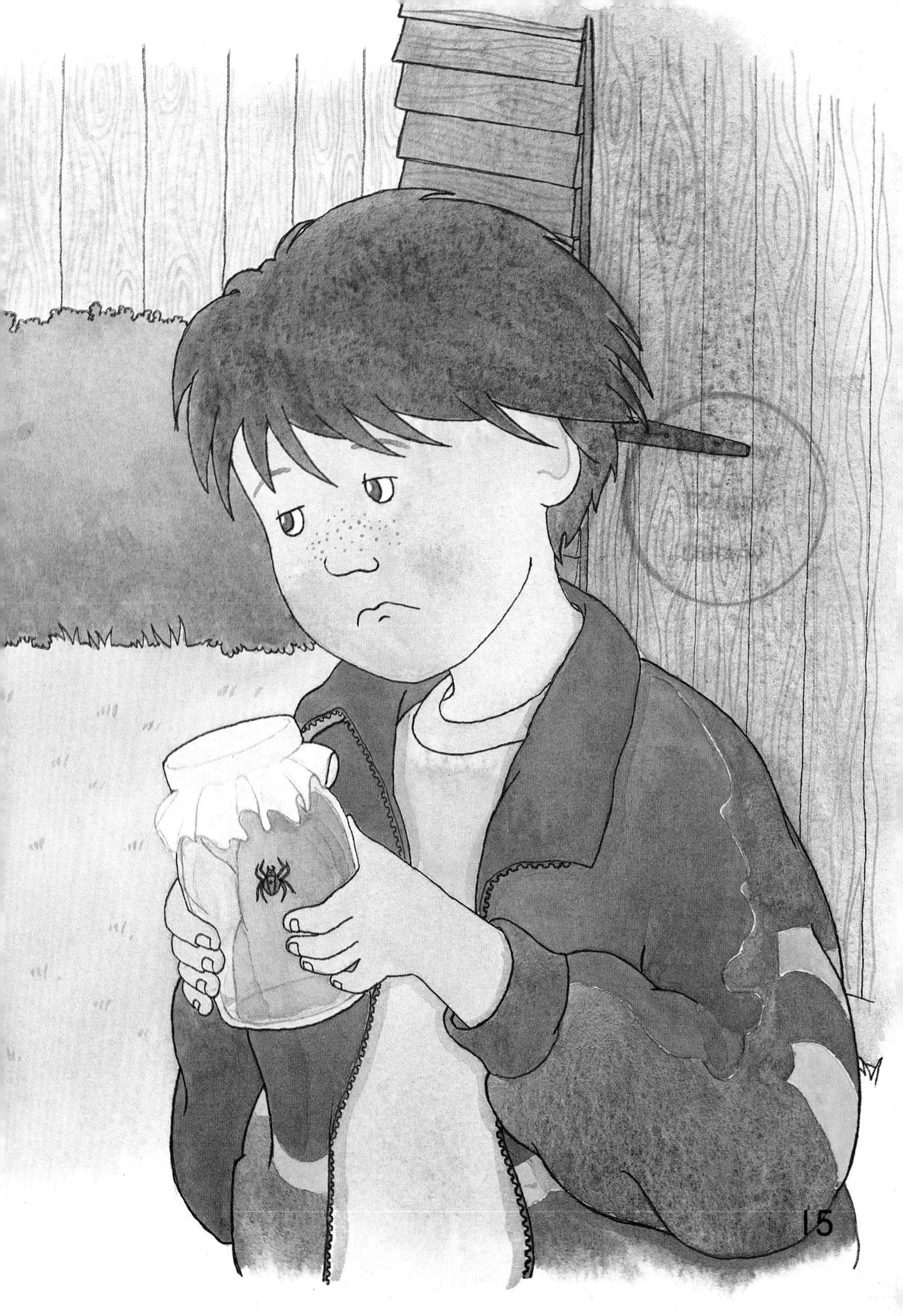

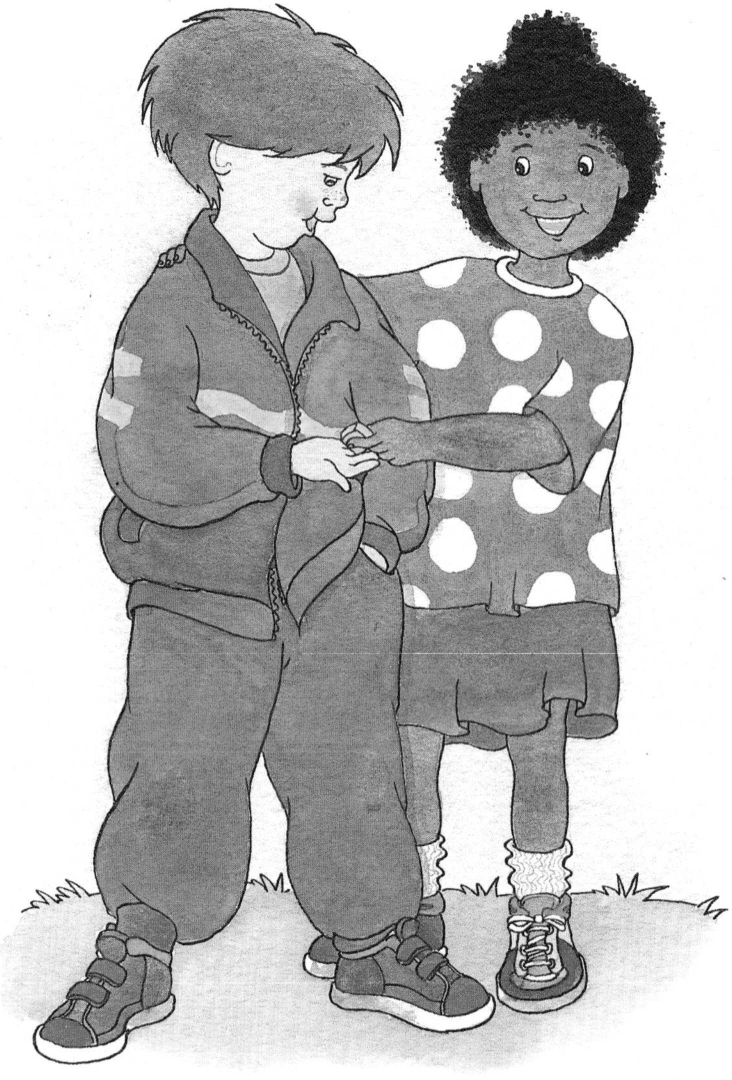

and she gave it to Sam.